Kyle

zahra

Zahra and Hanifa, Anisa, Zineera, Maryam, Rania, Amira,
Rafael, Waris, Zoya, Sabrina, Ismail, Inaya, Hawwa, Khadeejah,
and ALL my cousins, especially the little ones:
Fatima, Muhammad, Maggie, Jack, Zainab, Ziyad.
May you always be helpful and kind!

– R. F.

To Cameron, Abby, Lily, and Jude.

– M. P.

Text © 2021 Reem Faruqi • Illustrations © 2021 Mikela Prevost

Published in 2021 by Eerdmans Books for Young Readers,
an imprint of Wm. B. Eerdmans Publishing Co., Grand Rapids, Michigan
www.eerdmans.com/youngreaders

29 28 27 26 25 24 23 22 21   1 2 3 4 5 6 7 8 9

Library of Congress Cataloging-in-Publication Data

Names: Faruqi, Reem, author. | Prevost, Mikela, illustrator.
Title: I can help / written by Reem Faruqi ; illustrated by Mikela Prevost.

Description: Grand Rapids, Michigan : Eerdmans Books for Young Readers,
    2021. | Audience: Ages 4-8. | Summary: "Zahra loves spending time with
    Kyle at school, but when her other classmates start teasing her for
    helping him she starts making choices she regrets"— Provided by
    publisher.
Identifiers: LCCN 2021000790 | ISBN 9780802855046 (hardcover)
Subjects: CYAC: Peer pressure—Fiction. | Kindness—Fiction. |
    Schools—Fiction.
Classification: LCC PZ7.1.F37 Iah 2021 | DDC [E]—dc23
LC record available at https://lccn.loc.gov/2021000790

Illustrations created with mixed media

I Can Help

WRITTEN BY
Reem Faruqi

ILLUSTRATED BY
Mikela Prevost

EERDMANS BOOKS FOR YOUNG READERS

GRAND RAPIDS, MICHIGAN

Just when the leaves are thinking of changing colors to look like the spices Nana cooks with, school starts.

There are 18 kids in my class. One of them is Kyle.

Kyle is great at drawing.
He always has his sketchbook open.

Kyle is great at drumming.
He always taps, taps, taps music during the breaks.

But Kyle is not great at reading.
He has trouble sounding out words.

Kyle isn't great at handwriting
or cutting or gluing either.

He needs someone to help him.

So every day, Ms. Underwood asks,
"Who will be Kyle's helper today?"

I always raise my hand. "I can help!"

Because Kyle is generous. He always shares his favorite chocolate chip cookies at lunch.

Because Kyle is funny. He is good at telling jokes.

Because Kyle is kind. He always smiles at me.

One day, Ms. Underwood chooses me to help.

We do such a good job that Ms. Underwood gives me not just one, but two thumbs up, and tells me, "Zahra, you really are a super helper, aren't you?"

I sit up nice and tall.

Kyle copies me, and we both laugh.

Later at recess, I take my turn on the swings.

When I'm all the way up high, I realize the leaves are no longer thinking about changing colors. They are already the colors of red pepper, cumin, and turmeric, the spices Nana uses.

Even though I'm at the top, I can hear
my classmates talking.

"Kyle is such a baby," says Tess.

"He looks weird," says Ashley.

I want to keep swinging, but I stop.

I want to stop listening, but my ears
listen harder.

Tess walks closer to the swings.
She looks like she wants a turn.

"Why do you help him?" asks Tess.

I want to explain why, but I don't.

I was going to give Tess
a turn on the swings, but
instead, I start swinging
as high as I can.

Why do I help him?
I try to stop thinking about
what Tess and Ashley said,
but I can't.

The next day, Ms. Underwood
asks me to help cut paper
for Kyle.

My hands feel heavy
as I pick up the scissors.

I am ready to cut.

I notice Tess and Ashley
looking at me.
Hard.

I put the paper down. My hands feel even heavier.

"Do it yourself!" I say, pushing the paper at Kyle.

I don't recognize my voice.

Kyle's face is stamped with worry.

"Zahra, I notice you aren't helping Kyle today," says Ms. Underwood.

I want to answer her, but I don't want my mean voice to come out.

I blink the right amount of blinks so I don't cry.

The next day, Ahmed helps Kyle.

I notice that Tess and Ashley are smiling at me.

I look at Ahmed helping.

I look at Kyle smiling and working.

I wish I could smile and work, but my lips aren't smiling today even if I try.

Does he know I still want to help him?

"You're mean now," Kyle says to me.

I notice that Tess and Ashley are watching me. Are they listening?

"So?" I still don't recognize my voice.

My face feels hot, my heart cold.

I stare down at my paper and pretend to focus.

Kyle keeps looking at me like
he doesn't know me.

I don't know me either.

I've never written my name
so slowly before.

I only look up when he walks away.

It's fall—again.

At my new school I have a chance to make
a new start.

Sometimes I find myself looking for Kyle,
even though I know he's not here.

It takes me a while to learn my way around.
I've never been in such a big school before.

One day when the trees are golden like tumeric, I see a girl.

She looks a little like Kyle.

Today, she looks lost.

Maybe she is new too.

I find my voice.
The voice that I know and am proud of.
The voice that's mine.

"Are you new?" I ask.

"I can help!"

Author's Note

Like Zahra, when I was in school, I sat with a classmate who sometimes needed a helper. I enjoyed helping him and became his friend. But when I was teased for helping him, I felt embarrassed and was mean to him. I regret my actions to this day. When I wanted to apologize, it was too late because I had moved away to a different school in a different continent.

From then on, I resolved to be kinder to those around me. Once I wasn't the new kid anymore, I tried to be extra welcoming to those students who were newer than me. I remembered how it felt to hurt someone, and I didn't want to be that person anymore.

When I was a teacher, I encouraged my students to not just say sorry to others, but to also apologize with their actions by doing something kind for the person that they hurt.

As an author, my tools are words. But while it can be easy to write about kindness, it can be harder to practice it. I hope my story inspires you to be better. If you see someone sitting alone at lunch, invite them to eat lunch with you. If you see someone struggling, help them. If you see someone new, welcome them.

Being kind is always the right decision.

Illustrator's Note

When I was 13, I was diagnosed with Juvenile Rheumatoid Arthritis and became seen as "different" from others because of my physical limitations. Some other students were kind and helpful, while others were not. Now as an adult, I remember both. I try to forgive those who were unkind. I know now that they were probably confused by and afraid of my situation, possibly fearing that what happened to me could happen to them. But I will be forever grateful to those that risked looking "weird" by showing me kindness.

As a former art teacher, I was able to see some of my students facing challenges not unlike my own. But the students that were kind and helped those that needed help, I still remember by name. I will be forever thankful to have witnessed such selfless kindness. I don't think they knew I was watching, but to give of yourself is to give hope to others.